this
Book belongs
to

For Joshua

Text © 1993 Francesca Simon
Illustrations © 1993 Nigel McMullen
Published exclusively for
Safeway
6 Millington Road, Hayes, Middx UB3 4AY
by Julia MacRae Books
a division of Random House
20 Vauxhall Bridge Road
London SW1V 2SA

First published 1993

Printed in Hong Kong
ISBN 1-85681-066-6

Papa Forgot

FRANCESCA **S**IMON & **N**IGEL **M**CMULLEN

SAFEWAY SUPERBOOKS

One night Harry's Mummy and Daddy went out.
Papa came to take care of Harry.

Papa is Harry's Daddy's Daddy.

"Now don't forget,"
said Harry's Mummy,
"Harry's food is in the fridge,
his slippers are under the bed,
and his paints are in the cupboard."
"Don't worry," said Papa,
"I won't forget."

"And don't forget,"
said Harry's Daddy,
"Harry's bathtime is at six o'clock,
and his bedtime is at seven."
"Don't worry," said Papa,
"I won't forget."

Harry and Papa waved goodbye.
Then Harry ate a tasty supper of
fish fingers, broccoli and ice-cream.

But Papa forgot . . .

... to put on Harry's bib.

Then Harry went into his bedroom and bounced on the bed.

But Papa forgot . . .

. . . to take off Harry's shoes.

Then Harry painted a lovely picture.

But Papa forgot . . .

. . . to put on Harry's smock.

The clock struck six. Bathtime.

But Papa forgot . . .

. . . to squeeze the bubble bath just once.

The clock struck seven. Bedtime.

But Papa forgot . . .

. . . to put Harry to bed.

Papa and Harry built a castle instead.

The clock struck eight. Papa and Harry went outside

and looked at the moon and the stars.

The clock struck nine. Papa put on a
record and they danced.

The clock struck ten. "What shall we do now?" asked Papa. But Harry didn't say anything.

Papa put Harry into his bed with Big Bear
and Baby Bear, and he *didn't* forget to
tuck them all in.

Just then Harry's Mummy and Daddy came home.
"Ssshh!" said Papa. "Harry is asleep."

"Did you have fun?"
whispered Harry's Mummy.
"Yes," said Papa.
"Was Harry a good boy?"
asked Harry's Daddy.
"Oh yes," said Papa, "the very best."
"Did you remember everything?"
asked Harry's Mummy.
"But of course!" said Papa.
"Papas never forget."

The
End